Let fear disappear,

is here!

Discover how the Squad go underwater
to investigate the latest mutant monster
to be spotted in Trashland.

It's time to fight crime with slime!

Collect all the cool cards and check out
the special website for more slimy stuff:

www.slimesquad.co.uk

Don't miss the rest of the series:

THE SLIME SQUAD VS THE FEARSOME FISTS
THE SLIME SQUAD VS THE TOXIC TEETH
THE SLIME SQUAD VS THE CYBER-POOS

Also available by the same author,
these fantastic series:

COWS IN ACTION

ASTROSAURS

ASTROSAURS ACADEMY

www.stevecolebooks.co.uk

THE SLIME SQUAD

vs

THE SUPERNATURAL SQUID

by Steve Cole

Illustrated by Woody Fox

RED FOX

THE SLIME SQUAD vs THE SUPERNATURAL SQUID
A RED FOX BOOK 978 1 862 30879 4

First published in Great Britain by Red Fox,
an imprint of Random House Children's Books
A Random House Group Company

This edition published 2010

1 3 5 7 9 10 8 6 4 2

The Random House Group Limited supports the Forest Stewardship
Council (FSC), the leading international forest certification
organization. All our titles that are printed on Greenpeace-approved
FSC-certified paper carry the FSC logo. Our paper procurement policy
can be found at www.rbooks.co.uk/environment.

Mixed Sources
Product group from well-managed
forests and other controlled sources
www.fsc.org Cert no. TT-COC-2139
FSC © 1996 Forest Stewardship Council

Set in Bembo Schoolbook

Red Fox Books are published by Random House Children's Books,
61–63 Uxbridge Road, London W5 5SA

www.kidsatrandomhouse.co.uk
www.rbooks.co.uk

Addresses for companies within The Random House Group Limited can
be found at: www.randomhouse.co.uk/offices.htm

THE RANDOM HOUSE GROUP Limited Reg. No. 954009

A CIP catalogue record for this book is available from
the British Library.

Printed in the UK by CPI Bookmarque, Croydon

To Matthew Roberts, David Ghanaiah,
Aidan Manley and Robbie Connolly

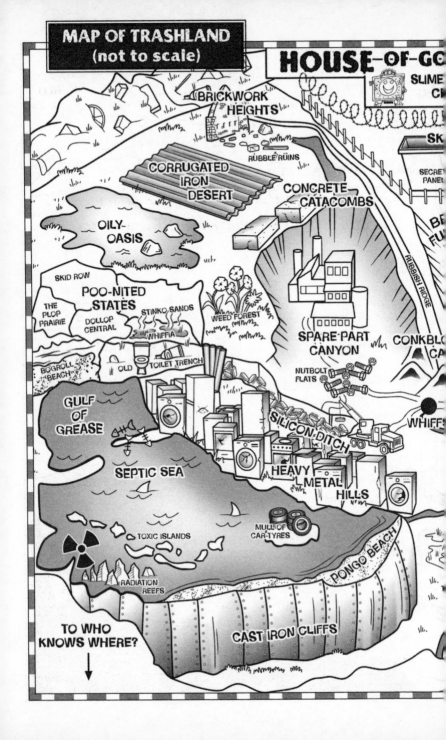

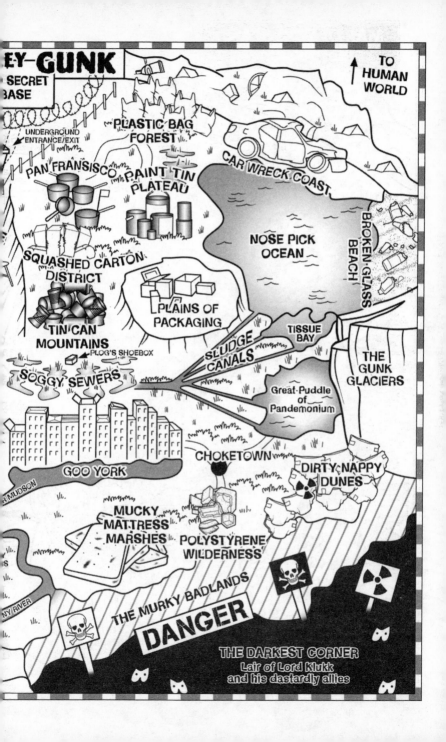

ONCE UPON A SLIME...

The old rubbish dump was far from anywhere. An enormous, mucky, rusty landscape of thousands of thrown-away things.

It had been closed for years. Abandoned. Forgotten.

And then Godfrey Gunk came along.

Godfrey wasn't just a mad scientist. He was a SUPER-BONKERS scientist! And he was very worried about the amount of pollution and rubbish in the world. His dream was to create marvellous mutant mini-monsters out of chemical goo – monsters who would clean up the planet by eating, drinking and generally devouring all types of trash.

So Godfrey bought the old rubbish dump as the perfect testing-ground and got to work.

Of course, he wanted to make good, friendly, peaceful monsters, so he was careful to keep the nastiest, most toxic chemicals separate from the rest. He worked for years and years . . .

And got nowhere.

In the end, penniless and miserable, Godfrey wrecked his lab, scattered his experiments all over the dump, and moved away, never to return.

But what Godfrey didn't know was that long ago, tons of radioactive sludge had been accidentally dumped here. And soon, its potent powers kick-started the monster chemistry the mad scientist had tried so hard to create!

Life began to form. Amazing mini-monsters sprang up with incredible speed.

Bold, inventive monsters, who made a wonderful, whiffy world for themselves from the rubbish around them – a world they named Trashland.

For many years, they lived and grew in peace. But then the radiation reached a lead-lined box in the darkest corner of the rubbish dump – the place where Godfrey had chucked the most toxic, dangerous gunk of all.

Slowly, very slowly, monsters began to grow here too.

Different monsters.

Evil monsters that now threaten the whole of Trashland.

Only one force for good stands against them. A small band of slightly sticky superheroes . . .

The Slime Squad!

Chapter One
ON PONGO BEACH

Plog the monster, leader of the Slime Squad, stood on the smelly shore with his furry ears folded forwards, shielding his eyes from the sun's glare. As he gazed out over the vast Septic Sea, a breeze blew in and ruffled his orangey fur.

"Ugh!" His long, ratlike snout twitched with the yucky whiff of the place. "No wonder they call this place Pongo Beach . . ."

But Plog knew this was no time to think of his nose.

He was on a mission.

Plog pulled a pair of battered binoculars from his waistcoat and peered about keenly. No boats were afloat on the oily water. The lumpy bulk of the Heavy Metal Hills glowed rustily to his right. The Cast-Iron Cliffs stretched behind in a wide, gleaming sweep, dwarfing the gunky brown shore.

Plog kept his eyes peeled for any sign of the glowing seal-like creatures – known as junkjacks – that the Slime Squad had come here to find. They were supposed to be Pongo Beach's only inhabitants.

Supposed to be . . .

Suddenly, Plog saw something large and dark come crashing out of the water just in front of him. He jumped backwards, slipped and fell to the gooey ground. The crab-like creature bore down on him – then shrugged off its wetsuit, spat out a snorkel and waved his powerful pincers in Plog's face. "Yoo-hooooo!"

"Danjo!" Plog complained. "You gave me a real shock."

"Better a real shock than a smelly sock," said Danjo, shaking water from his three sturdy legs and adjusting his golden shorts. "Although I did find one

of those on my undersea scouting swim."
He peeled a large blue sock from under
his armpit. "Would you like that too?"

"No, thanks," said Plog. "I'm trying to
give them up." He scrambled back to his
feet. "Did you see any junkjacks under
there? Or any bad guys?"

"It's so dark and
gloopy I couldn't see
much at all." Danjo
tossed away the
sock and
stretched.
"Maybe we
should just
sunbathe for a
bit?"

"Good idea,"
called Zill, a
black-and-white
skunky poodle monster in a gold
leotard. She waved at them from a
ledge high up on the Cast-Iron Cliffs.

4

"I've taken a look from above as you asked, Fur-boy. Lovely view of Goo York from up here, and of the whole Poo-nited States . . ." She coughed out a long gooey strand of slime, fixed it to the side of the cliff, then gripped it with all six of her legs and abseiled down. "It looks like there's a junkjack camp further up the beach, but it's deserted. They've probably all gone fishing." Reaching the beach, she put on a cool pair of shades. "Until they get back, let's chill out. Life in the Slime Squad is so tough, we could use a break."

5

Danjo grinned. "That's for sure!"

Plog nodded with feeling. Being a slime-sloshing superhero was hard work. Together with their friend Furp – a technological whizz-frog  who was also scouting the area right now – Plog, Zill and Danjo battled constantly to stop evil mutant-monsters from taking over Trashland. Led by a shadowy mastermind who went by the name of Lord Klukk, the monsters were getting rougher and tougher all the time.

Luckily, besides their natural bravery, agility and freaky slime-charged powers, the Squaddies had one other advantage over their fearsome foes – their boss, the All-Seeing PIE. This super-duper super-computer kept a close

6

watch over Trashland and whenever he picked up on something dodgy, he sent the Squad to investigate. And PIE had sent them here to the shores of the Septic Sea because he sensed that something *really* dodgy was kicking off . . .

But what?

"Come on, Plog," urged Danjo, lying down on the stinky sand. "Chill out and warm up." He squirted himself with hot slime from his left pincer and rubbed it into his crusty skin. "This stuff's not only great for bringing down bad guys — it makes a wicked sun tan lotion!"

"What's this?" Furp the frog-monster hopped into sight, his round metal pants rattling as he did so. "Sleeping on the job?"

7

"Catching some rays," Zill retorted.
"A quick holiday."

"Sunbathing? Puh!" Furp turned up his nose. "Give me a nice shady lab and some slime to work on any day . . ."

Plog smiled. As well as being a big-brained superhero who could stick to any surface, Furp was an expert on all things slimy. "I suppose you didn't see any junkjacks either?"

"Not one," Furp admitted, his golden crash helmet sparkling in the sunshine. "So while we wait for them to show, I'll just pop back to the Slime-mobile and finish perfecting my 'Slime-Power Plus'."

 Zill peered at him over her shades. "Your what?"

"Slime-Power Plus is a special serum packed with raw, slimy energy,"

Furp explained. "It can boost any power supply – batteries, engines, *anything* – and will make them run better, brighter, faster and longer."

Plog nodded thoughtfully. "Furp, this Slime-Power Plus wouldn't have anything to do with that massive, top-secret gadget you made me and Danjo load up before we left, would it?"

Furp chuckled. "Just you wait and see, my dear Plog." He hopped away to the Slime-mobile, their invisible monster-truck mobile-HQ parked further along the beach. "Just you wait!"

"There you go, Fur-boy," said Zill. "If the All-Seeing PIE didn't want us to take a break he would have told us through his radio-link in Furp's helmet.

Now, take your shoes off. Feel the sand between your toes."

Plog glanced down at the big iron, water-filled boots he wore and shot her a look. "You know that if my feet ever dry out they start oozing the most revolting, smelly, gloopy slime in the world!"

"Well then, come paddling in the sea with me." Zill jumped up and waded into the water on her hind legs, her tail wagging. "Ooooh, I haven't been to the seaside in ages . . ."

Plog saw the smile on her face and decided to join her.

He pulled off his
boots and ran
quickly into the
gloopy water; it
lapped at his
fur, its oily
surface alive
with rainbow
patterns.

Then,
suddenly, he
caught a dart
of orange
movement. "Look,
Zill – a goopfish."

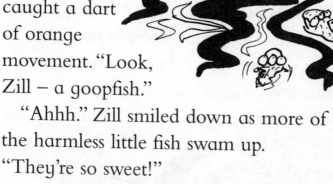

"Ahhh." Zill smiled down as more of
the harmless little fish swam up.
"They're so sweet!"

Plog looked around and frowned. The
water was thick with little orange
shapes now. "I've never seen so many."

Zill lowered her snout to the water.
"Hello, little fishies – OW!"

Two little goopfish were greedily chomping on her nose!

"Hey!" Plog quickly brushed them off – but as he did so, they latched onto his fingers. "Ouch!" He gasped even louder as maybe fifty more of the little swimmers bit into his furry bottom. "ARGH!"

"They've gone crazy," Zill gasped as the savage goopfish overwhelmed her, dragging her down beneath the churning water. "Get out of here, Fur-boy – it's like they want to eat us!"

Chapter Two
JUNKJACKS AHOY!

"Zill!" Plog pushed more of the crazed goopfish away as he grabbed desperately for his friend to stop her sinking under. "Danjo, help!"

"On the case!" Danjo was already splashing into the water. Almost at once, a small white jellyfish leaped out of the water and landed on his head.

"Hey, get off!" Danjo protested as its tentacles whipped round his eyestalks. "That stings!"

"The sea-life around here's gone berserk," Plog shouted as more goopfish tried to chow down on his ears. Finally, he lifted Zill out of the water by her tail and hurled her over his shoulder. She landed in a heap on the beach, and the goopfish fell twitching away from her.

"Thanks," Zill panted. But as she wiped her eyes, she could see both Plog and Danjo floundering in the thick, dark water. Swiftly, she spat out a thick slime-line and looped it around their middles. Then she tugged with all her strength and tried to reel them in, like an angler making the biggest catch of her life. SPLOOSH! Plog was pulled clear of the water and landed with a crash on the shore. But the goopfish had

14

dragged Danjo down and he'd slipped through Zill's slimy lasso.

"Come on," Zill urged Plog, "we must go back in and help him."

"I think I'll be able to help Danjo more by staying *out* of the water." Plog held his ugly bare feet up to the hot sun - because as soon as his feet dried out, his natural slime began to ooze with super-smelly results! Zill choked and held her nose as 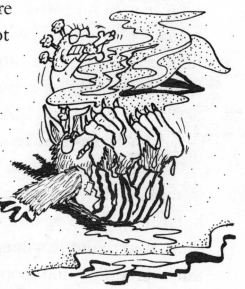 stinking, bright-yellow goop trickled from his toes to his heels like melting ice cream running down a cone. Then Plog used his tail to propel himself through the air — landing feet-first in the sea with a colossal SPLOSH beside the crimson crab-monster. And as his ultra-toxic tootsies bubbled in the water, the goopfish and jellyfish broke off their attack, stunned into submission.

"Whoa, thanks!" Danjo popped out of the water like a big crabby cork and Plog helped him wade back to the beach. "I'm not sure which was worse," he joked, "that aqua-attack or your slimy rescue . . ."

Plog grinned and quickly put his boots back on. "You're welcome!"

"Look at my leotard," Zill complained. "Now it's full of holes."

Danjo peered at his golden shorts. "My waistband has been chewed too."

Just then, Furp opened the Slime-mobile's invisible door and hopped outside. "What's all the noise? I was just loading some Slime-Power Plus into my secret invention when I heard you shout. Did I miss something?"

"Oh, no," said Zill, rolling her eyes. "We were just enjoying a swim – with some killer sea-life."

"What got into those things?" Plog wondered. "Goopfish are normally sweet, harmless little things – but this lot tried to chomp us and drown us. And I never heard of jellyfish attacking passing monsters before."

"The really weird thing is, they gave me no bother at all when I went for my swim earlier," said Danjo.

"That *is* odd," Plog agreed. "I wonder what changed their mood and made them so hungry?"

Furp was looking past him, out to the horizon. "Perhaps *they* can tell us."

Plog, Zill and Danjo turned – and got a shock. An unlikely fleet of sardine-tin boats had floated into sight and was drawing closer, each one steered by a crew of pale, bottle-nosed seal-monsters whose skin seemed to glow in the sunlight. Dressed in rags, their scaly snouts raised to the wind, they rowed with power and precision and lolly-stick oars, as though born to a life on the water.

"These must be the junkjacks," Plog breathed. "We couldn't find them – but they've found us."

The junkjacks soon reached the shore, using ropes and grappling hooks to drag their tin-ships out of the dangerous water.

Plog watched as one junkjack – bigger, more grizzled and glowing a slightly brighter shade of green than the others – slithered across the beach towards him.

"Ha-harrr," called the approaching monster in a gruff, pirate-y voice. "I is Dolofin, leader of the junkjacks."

"We've heard you're in trouble," said Zill, "'so we've come to help."

"We're the Slime Squad," Furp added proudly.

"Us knows who you is." Dolofin smiled. "Even in this far corner of the land, us has heard of Zill, Danjo, Furp and . . ."

"Plog," said Plog.

"Bog, yes." Dolofin nodded. "You is Bog."

"No, *Plog*."

"Fog?"

"PLOG!"

"No need to shout. I understand. You is Nog." As Plog sighed, Dolofin turned to the others. "Pardon my manners.

20

How do you all be doing?"

Danjo pointed towards the sea, which seemed calm again now. "To be honest, not so good after fighting the fish of fury in there."

Dolofin nodded grimly. "Us thought us heard a commotion across the ocean. That's why us came to see." He sighed. "Commotions happen a lot round here – right, lads?"

The ragged band of junkjacks behind him muttered and nodded.

"The seaweed us eat is all disappearing," one called. "Us has to go further and further across the Septic Sea to find it."

"And the sea's turned against us!" wailed another. "The goopfish try to nibble us. Jellyfish and sponges try to splat us."

21

"I was even savaged by a septic sea cucumber the other day," said Dolofin, holding up a scratched fin.

Furp frowned. "But the wildlife isn't angry all the time."

"No," Dolofin agreed. "Sometimes it's nice as pie."

"It would be nicer IN a pie," Danjo declared.

"Not for us," said Dolofin. "Us can't nosh nothing but seaweed. If us does, us gets the deadly screaming wibble-trots and dies."

Plog didn't know what the deadly screaming wibble-trots were, and he wasn't keen to find out.

"And that's not the worst of it," cried a small, wrinkled junkjack. "Tell them about the squid, Dolofin!"

Plog frowned. "What squid?"

"You might be thinking us is bonker-crackers," said Dolofin, "but us is being haunted by a giant ghost-squid!"

Furp looked doubtful. "Couldn't it be a real squid?"

Dolofin shook his head. "Us has seen it vanish before our eyes, leaving only a few splats of gloopiness to prove it were ever there at all."

"It lurks in the darkness," twittered the small junkjack.

"It makes our precious seaweed disappear," cried another.

Plog shivered. An air of mystery and menace had suddenly settled over Pongo Beach.

"It all started one dark night, months ago," Dolofin went on in a low, spooky voice. "The Cast-Iron Cliffs started a-rumbling. There was a grinding and a trembling and a rattling night after night, as if furious phantoms were shaking the cliffs from the inside. And when it finally stopped – that's when the squid appeared for the first time."

"Most mysterious," murmured Furp.

"Us reckons the rumbling in the cliffs was the squid travelling up from the ghostly underworld," called the wrinkly junkjack. "And now it has turned the other sea-life into its scary servants – set on our destruction!"

"But there's no such thing as ghosts," Danjo protested.

"Believe what you like," said Dolofin. "But us junkjacks has seen that squid coming at us from out of the darkness . . . tentacles a-trembling, giant and stripy and hungering for our very souls . . ." He shrugged. "Or possibly for seaweed. Arrr, either our very souls, or seaweed – one of the two."

Zill whispered to Plog: "He's a looper!"

"But there's something weird going on here," Plog hissed back. "I'll bet my mask that Lord Klukk and his evil monsters are behind it. And if they are, it's not only the junkjacks who are in danger – it's the whole of Trashland!"

Chapter Three

SOMETHING IN THE WATER

"Well, no point moaning on," said Dolofin gruffly. "Us has got our packing up to do."

Zill frowned at the soft-glowing junkjack. "Packing up?"

"Arr. Since that supernatural squid chases us away whenever us tries to gather our precious seaweed, and the rest of the sea-life keeps attacking our ships, us be starving and scared the whole time ..." Dolofin sniffed and wiped a tear from

26

his eye. "Most junkjacks have already cleared off to the Nosepick Ocean, far to the north. Us was the last lot to stay here. But now . . ."

"Dolofin, this is your home," said Plog. "You can't let anyone bully you into moving away – not even mysterious phantoms."

Danjo clenched his pincers. "Especially when the Slime Squad are here to make a mystery *history*." He looked around at his friends. "Right, guys?"

"Right," Zill agreed. "But how can we go poking around deep under the sea? Look what happened when we had a quick paddle – we were almost nibbled to death!"

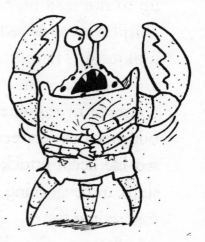

But Furp just grinned. "Plog, Danjo – you remember that massive, top-secret gadget I made you load on board the Slime-mobile? Kindly unload it again." He clapped his slimy hands in excitement. "My creation is ready to be revealed!"

Plog and Danjo duly squeezed aboard the Slime-mobile – which wasn't easy because the secret invention took up a massive amount of space. With some difficulty, some scraped invisible paintwork, and a few "oooh"s and "ahhh"s from the gathered junkjacks, they staggered off the Slime-mobile and dropped the huge bundle – wrapped up in an even huger blanket – lengthways onto the sand. Furp hopped over, grabbed one end of the blanket – and yanked it away . . . to reveal a large, dented metal canister. "Ta-daaaa!"

Dolofin stared at him. "What be that, then?"

"It's a big can," said Zill, unimpressed. "With dents in."

Furp shook his head. "No, no, no, my dear Zill – my invention is simply in stealth mode at the moment." He pressed a tiny hidden button on the side, and a huge, pointed nose-cone with a glass windscreen slid out from one end.

A large, rusty compartment shot out from the other. Graceful fins popped out and locked into place – one on each side and another on the roof. Finally, a pair of powerful jets poked out from the gadget's rear.

"Presenting the most sensational, slime-propelled sub-sea super-craft in the world," Furp declared. "I call it the Slime Sub . . . and with it, no undersea adventure is beyond our reach!" He patted it fondly, and one of the fins fell off with a clatter. "Oops! Some of the slime-glue hasn't quite set yet."

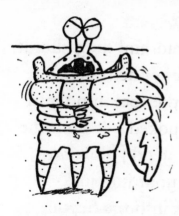

Danjo frowned. "You seriously want us to go looking underwater for giant nasty ghost-squid in this thing?"

"Of course," cried Furp. "Once I've added Power-Slime Plus to the fuel tank it'll go like the clappers! And I'm *fairly* sure the glue is waterproof . . ."

Zill groaned. Danjo shook his head. But Plog just smiled. "There you go, Dolofin – next to this bucket of bolts, a ghostly squid isn't so scary, right?"

Dolofin did not smile back . . .

Within the hour, Danjo had fixed the fin and Furp had finished his safety checks. The Slime Squad got into their diving gear, good to go.

Furp turned to the gently glowing Dolofin. "If you and your junkjacks could kindly shove us into the Septic Sea once we're inside, that would be a big help."

"Arrr," said Dolofin doubtfully. "Well, I don't expect none of us will ever see you again, as you will surely sink to the bottom of the ocean and die — but it was nice knowing you."

"Don't say goodbye just yet." Plog climbed a wonky ladder onto the roof and lifted the entry hatch. "We'll be back."

He studied
the inside of
the sub. From
corner to
corner it was
stuffed with
machines and
flashing lights.
Wires hung
down from the

ceiling like thick cobwebs. It would be a
snug fit for four of them.

Zill, the Squad's top driver, was
already squeezed up in the front, getting
to grips with the controls. Plog climbed
down and sat behind her in the
weapons zone – he had been put in
charge of the submarine's built-in slime-
shooters, ready to give any bad guys a
serious squirt if they tried to attack.
Danjo shimmied down beside him and
took his place beside a porthole, ready
to act as lookout. Finally, Furp squeezed

in at the back close to the Slime Sub's engines. He held a spanner in one hand and a screwdriver in the other, ready to tinker with the jets if they started playing up.

"Everyone ready?" asked Furp, and his friends nodded. "Right, then – let's move out!" He banged noisily on the ceiling. The Slime Sub lurched and rocked as Dolofin and his luminous junkjacks hefted it up and hurled it into the sea. *KER-SPLASH!*

Zill hit the starter button. With a strange squealing, rumbling noise, the whole sub began to shake. "Engines firing," she reported. "We're off!"

Plog felt his tummy tingle as they descended into dark water, ready to face the unknown.

Long minutes passed as the sub chugged onwards. Zill switched on the headlights, but the water was so thick with pollution and goo it was hard to see much. A giant human boot loomed up like a sinister shadow. A torn carrier bag floated past like some weird sea-creature.

"How do the junkjacks ever find seaweed in this muck?" Danjo wondered.

"They have luminous bodies to light their way," Furp explained.

"Maybe their light attracts the supernatural squid too," said Zill nervously. "In which case, our headlights might do the same . . ."

BAMMMM!

Something large and hard smashed into the Slime Sub, sending it into a spin. Zill was thrown from her seat as the controls spat sparks and the headlights switched off. Danjo lost his balance and crashed to the floor. Plog was sent flying backwards into Furp, squashing him against the back wall.

Danjo sat up and smothered the burning controls with a squirt of slime-ice. "What did we hit?" he shouted.

"I can't see." Zill grabbed the blackened wheel, swinging the sub from side to side. "Furp, can you fix the headlights?"

The frog-monster crawled out from under Plog and fiddled with some wires poking up from the damaged control panel. A single headlight flickered into feeble life . . .

And suddenly the Squaddies could see a huge eye glaring in at them, bloodshot and yellow with a big black centre. The rubbery skin around it was blotchy and pale.

Plog's jaw dropped and his ears shot up in the air as he stared in horror. "IT'S THE SUPERNATURAL SQUID!"

The Squaddies watched in alarm as the colossal squid's single eye narrowed. With a twitch of rubbery flesh it flicked out fat, trailing tentacles towards the Slime Sub.

"That thing's going to get us!" Zill cried.

"It'll get something else first." Plog jabbed a furry finger on the slime-squirter's fire button. "A slimy surprise!"

SLOOSH! Stinging slime sprayed out from the little ship's cannons. The creature retreated into the gloom, but its powerful tentacles closed around the Slime Sub and started to squeeze.

Danjo's crimson shell turned pale with fright. "It'll squash us like an old can."

Plog opened fire again with the slime-squirters, but the tentacles didn't budge. "I don't know even know if I'm hitting it!"

Furp yanked down a tangle of wires from the ceiling. "Slime-Power Plus is designed to boost any power source. Perhaps it can boost our remaining headlight so you can see what you're shooting . . ."

He poured his special slimy mixture over the wires that linked the headlight to the sub's batteries. *VIMMM!* The dim light suddenly became brighter than the sun. And in the sudden flare of whiteness, Plog saw the monster's cruel, hooked beak opening wide in front of them, ready to crunch down on the cockpit of the little craft . . .

Chapter Four

DEEP-SEA DREAD

The Squaddies screamed as the massive mouth widened to swallow the sub. But then suddenly – PLOOP!

The giant squid disappeared.

"What happened?" breathed Danjo. "That thing had us where it wanted us. Then it just vanished like . . . like . . ."

"Like a ghost," said Zill, her eyes wide and fearful. "It really IS a supernatural squid!"

"And here come its scary servants," said Danjo grimly, pointing a pincer at a hundred little orange shapes glittering in the headlight's glare. "Goopfish alert!"

Plog was almost knocked off his feet as the fish slammed into the Slime Sub and a terrible scraping sound started up. "Looks like they're in a rotten mood again – they're trying to chew their way inside!"

"I'll try to get us back to the surface." Zill struggled with the controls as the goopfish swarmed about the sub, smothering the light. Tiny dents started showing in the side walls. Then sponges squelched against the windscreen alongside big white jellyfish whipping their tendrils, trying to crack the glass.

Desperately, Plog fired the slime-squirters. SLOOSH! The furious creatures fell away, sizzling and steaming.

But then the battered sub rocked even more fiercely than before, as further thick tentacles snaked past the portholes. Danjo groaned. "The squid is back!"

Furp gulped. "It must have reappeared behind us – and now it's grabbed hold!"

Plog fired the slime-squirters wildly. A massive dent appeared in the ceiling as the squid lashed out angrily. "We've got to break its grip."

"No good," Zill shouted, as more goopfish swarmed over the sub, trying to tear it apart. "We don't have enough power to pull free."

"I'll use the last of my Slime-Power Plus to top up the fuel tank!" Furp wrestled with the engine's inspection hatch cover. "Help me get this thing off, Danjo!"

Danjo quickly wrenched away the cover with his powerful pincers, allowing Furp to pour the last drops from his bottle into a greasy hole in the metalwork. "There might just be enough left to give us an energy boo—oooooooooooost!"

With a whopping *WHOOSH!* the very last drips of the Slime-Power Plus did their job – stoking the engines with

raw, super-charged slime. The
sudden power-rush sent the
sub shooting up through the
water like an atomic
salmon fired from a deep-
sea catapult. As they
finally broke the surface
of the Septic Sea and
went flying up into
the air, Plog was
thrown against a
porthole. He
glimpsed a
squashy, bloated
body being
dragged along
behind them
– the squid
was still
hanging
on . . .

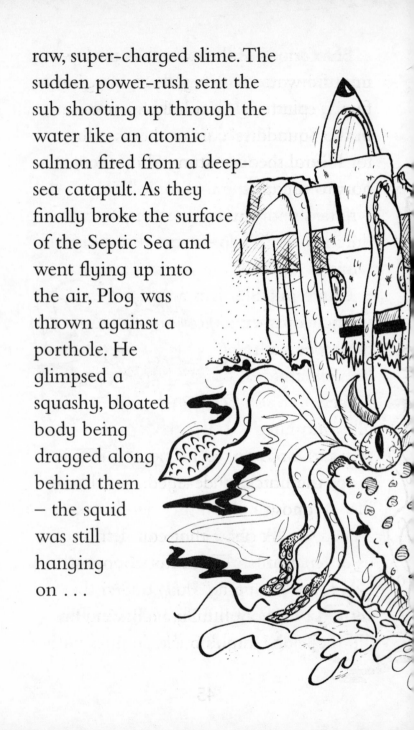

But then the sub crashed back down into the water with a jolt. The engines finally spluttered to a halt. Silence rang in the Squaddies' ears as they sat there for several seconds, stunned by their narrow escape.

Then Plog threw open the hatch in the sub's roof, climbed out and looked wildly around in the warm sunlight.

The Septic Sea was calm and still. The savage, super-enormous squid had disappeared.

Zill climbed out and stood beside him. "Vanished again," she murmured.

Danjo poked his head through the hatch, wide-eyed. "Just like a ghost."

"A ghost that can turn peaceful fish into ravenous monsters," Furp added thoughtfully, balancing on Danjo's back.

45

"There was nothing ghostly about that squid's grip on the sub," Plog reminded him, pointing to the deep dents in the Slime Sub's roof.

Then all four Squaddies jumped as a group of goopfish popped their heads out of the water. But the little creatures only smiled before swimming calmly on their way.

"The fish seem back to normal again now," Plog observed. "Perhaps they only turn nasty when the squid's around."

"Ghostly mind control?" Danjo looked worried. "I wonder why that squid decided to let us go?"

"Perhaps this was just a warning," said Furp. "A show of squiddy strength." He sighed. "In any case, we'd better get back to Pongo Beach and try to repair the Slime Sub."

Zill's tail drooped. "And tell the junkjacks that we're as helpless as they are . . ."

The damaged Slime Sub limped back to shore. As Pongo Beach came into sight, Plog saw a gang of junkjacks were busy packing away their camp as Dolofin barked out instructions. Crates, chests and even some of the sardine-tin boats were being loaded onto wagons made from driftwood and cotton reels.

As the sub washed up on the beach, Dolofin slithered to join them. "So!" he said, surveying the ship's battle-scars. "I be thinking you found that ghostly squid us warned you about, eh, Nog?"

"That's *Plog*," said Plog. "But you're right, we certainly did."

"And it nearly squished us," Zill added.

"Arrr." The old junkjack gave a long, bubbling sigh through his pointed snout. "Well, thanks for trying to help. But now you know there be nothing anyone can do. Us'll be off soon . . ." He turned and slid away across the shore.

Furp watched him go sadly. "I think it's time we called into the All-Seeing PIE and told him all we know."

Plog sighed. "That'll be a short call!"

While Danjo got busy beating out the dents in the sub, Zill, Plog and Furp talked to PIE in the Slime-mobile.

48

Furp plugged his special crash helmet into one of the monster truck's control panels and an image of the peerlessly powerful computer appeared on a screen.

"Ah, there you are," PIE boomed. "My sensors saw you go into the Septic Sea but there was a lot of interference. Did you run up against any supernatural squid?"

"I'll say." Plog quickly filled him in on what had happened.

Several exclamation-marks appeared on PIE's screen. "A most mysterious business," he concluded. "Although I don't know if Lord Klukk is behind it or not. He wants to conquer Trashland, but squid are watery creatures – surely even supernatural ones can't float out to invade towns and cities?"

"I hope not," said Zill with a shudder.

"Well, I will keep my sensors peeled for any sign of the squid beyond the Septic Sea," said PIE. "In the meantime, we must find out the truth behind these squid. You must capture one."

The fur-knots on the back of Zill's neck shivered. "That won't be easy."

"Since when did the Slime Squad do easy?" PIE boomed tetchily. "Now, fix the Slime Sub and get on with it!"

With PIE's instructions ringing in their ears, the Slime Squad got busy. Furp designed some new slimy defences for the sub, and Zill and Plog built them from his plans while Danjo worked hard to strengthen the sub's metal shell.

The junkjacks, meanwhile, finished packing their possessions.

As the sun started to sink in the sky, Plog and Zill looked down at the long, rusty bazooka-like  weapon they'd constructed.

"Ready for a test, Fur-boy?" Zill winked and aimed the bazooka at the Cast-Iron Cliffs. BLAMM! A bolt of green goo struck them with a sizzling explosion and a cloud of green smoke, blasting a shallow crater in the stretch of metal.

"Woo-hoo!" cheered Danjo from the water's edge. "That should give our ghostly pal something to chew on!"

"What if it just disappears again?" Plog wondered.

"That's where this slime-net comes in!" cried Furp. He bounced out of the Slime-mobile with a huge net knitted together from Zill's slime lines. "If the squid does its vanishing act when we open fire, it will soon come back to get us, right? And when it does . . ." He hurled the net through the air and it spread out like a gigantic holey blanket over the whiffy sand.

"We catch it in this!"

"But we'll be inside the sub," said Plog. "Won't we get a bit wet trying to throw that outside?"

Furp shook his head. "We can load it into the bazooka and fire it at the touch of a button – once Danjo's mounted it on the roof."

"Shouldn't take long," Danjo assured him. He leaned on the Slime Sub, which was looking slick and shiny even in the gathering gloom. "I've already fitted it with ultra-hard, dent-proof slime-shields for extra protection. Next time we run into that ghost-squid, we'll be ready."

Plog was about to agree – when suddenly he saw long, twitching tentacles curl out from the shallow water beside the sub. "Look out, Danjo," he shouted. "Ready or not – SQUID ALERT!"

Chapter Five

TENTACLES OF TERROR

Even as Danjo turned, two of the tentacles gripped hold of the Slime Sub and dragged it away into the forbidding water.

"Get off!" Danjo bellowed. "I spent all day working on that!" He fired hot and cold slime at the bloated, billowing beast as it rose from the shallows – but then another twisting tendril grabbed him around the waist. "Let go!" he groaned, struggling wildly as he was lifted high into the air.

"Danjo!" cried Zill, spitting out a slime-line with a flick of her head. "Catch hold!"

Danjo reached out, but the squid yanked him away and the line fell short.

Plog grabbed the bazooka and splashed into the water. But the ghostly creature was already sinking back into the sea.

"Be careful!" called Zill. "You might hit Danjo!"

BLAMM! Plog fired at the spot where he'd last seen the squid — but a horde of goopfish bit at his legs and a sea cucumber struck him on the nose.

He dropped the bazooka and fell back onto the beach, kicking off the crazed fish. "Zill, Furp – get the net."

"What be going on?" Dolofin slithered up and peered into the gloom – then gasped. "Great salty sea-cakes. That be yon Danjo!"

"Glad you noticed!" spluttered Danjo from the water.

"It's too dark to see properly," Zill complained, as she and Furp struggled with the net.

"I'll hit the headlights," Plog panted, bundling into the Slime-mobile. Twin beams of brilliance shone out onto the thrashing water, revealing Danjo, the sub and—

PLOOP! At once the tentacles disappeared.

"It's gone," said Danjo weakly,
clinging onto the sub as it bobbed in the
water. "Done its ghost act again." But
his friends' relief didn't last — as suddenly
Danjo was dragged back under. "It's got
hold of my legs!" he gasped.

"Throw the net!" Zill commanded.
With Dolofin's help,
she and Furp
threw the
slime-net. But
the crazed
goopfish and
sponges tore it
to pieces the
moment it
touched the water.

"The Slime Sub!"
Plog shouted helplessly. "Get inside it,
Danjo. NOW!"

Danjo reached for the sub and dug
his pincers into the roof. Kicking and
struggling against gobbling goopfish as

well as the terrible tentacles, he managed to open the hatch – just as a huge wave of filthy water slooshed over his head. The next moment, both he and the sub were lost from sight.

"Oh no!" Zill wailed. "The squid's disappeared again – and taken Danjo with it!"

"And the Slime Sub too." Furp stared at the still waters in disbelief. "It's almost as if it knew we'd made weapons and defences to help us catch it – and stole the whole lot before we could!"

"I just hope Danjo got inside the sub before . . . before . . . " Zill wiped a tear from her eye. "Oh, he *must* be all right!"

"He's a strong swimmer," Plog reassured her. "And without our sub, we need strong swimmers to go after him." He looked hopefully at Dolofin. "Well?"

"That grisly ghost never came so close ashore before," said Dolofin with a shiver. "I is betting it be after the last of our precious seaweed."

"There be nowhere safe from it," wailed the wrinkly junkjack.

"Look at this!" Furp picked up a small orange fish and a pale, blubbery scrap from the edge of the shore. "The

goopfish are friendly again, and I think *this* is a bit of squid tentacle! Plog, you must have blown a bit of it off when you fired the bazooka."

59

"See?" Plog turned to the junkjacks. "If we still had our Slime Sub I'll bet we could deal with that thing for good."

Zill looked pleadingly at Dolofin. "But without your in-built glow to guide us in the water we'll never find Danjo *or* the sub."

"What if it steals our seaweed while us be gone?" Dolofin protested. "Without it, us'll starve to death on the way to Nosepick Ocean."

"And what happens if you find supernatural squid there too?" Plog demanded. "Where will you run to then?"

Furp nodded. "We are here to help you – but you have to help yourselves too."

"And as for taking care of your seaweed, I've got a brilliant idea," said Zill, pointing to the Cast-Iron Cliffs. "See that crater we blasted over there? If we fire again and make it a bit deeper we can create a special cave for your seaweed. You can keep it safely out of the way for as long as you like."

Plog grabbed his bazooka. "I'll get up there now and start blasting – if you'll guide us on this rescue mission."

The junkjacks looked at each other nervously. But Dolofin nodded and glowed a fraction brighter. "Us'll be rescuing ourselves as well as your pal." He placed his flipper in Plog's hand and shook. "It's a deal!"

"Perhaps there's enough of the net left to use as a ladder." Furp splashed into the water, still lit by the Slime-mobile's headlights – and frowned. "Funny. Where the squid was hiding, it's left some sort of cloudy goop behind."

"Arr," said Dolofin. "It be ghostly goo."

"Maybe." Furp pulled a test tube from his pants and scooped up a little. "Or maybe this is what the squid uses to make itself disappear . . ."

"Well, right now it's Danjo who's disappeared," Zill reminded him. "And we need to get him back. So the sooner we get this cave built. . ."

"Yes, of course," Furp said distractedly.

He pulled out the remains of the net and threw it across to Plog. "Use this to climb up to the crater. I'd better run some tests on this goo in the lav-lab right away! It might help us follow the squid's trail. Excuse me . . ."

Plog watched Furp hop off to the Slime-mobile. "Let's hope he learns something that will help us find the squid faster." He hurled the net up at the cliff and it caught on a twisted spur of metal. "Come on – let's get climbing!"

Chapter Six

CAPTIVES IN THE CLIFFS

Plog and Zill soon reached the hole in the side of the cliff. The wall of iron reflected the moon's pale disc, and with its light to guide him, Plog took aim with the bazooka. BLAMM! With a big green splat and a cloud of seething smoke, the hole was blown deeper into the cliff side, making a shallow cave. BLAMM! He fired again, and the sizzling slime ate deeper still. "There."

"I'll just quickly smooth out some of the rough edges," said Zill. "We don't want the junkjacks hurting themselves when they climb up here to grab their supper." She banged about with the hammer . . . and suddenly something cold splashed into her face. "Urph!" she spluttered. "What's that?"

Plog pulled her clear. "*Water's* that, you mean." A jet of liquid was squirting out from a little hole in the metal. "I

don't get it – this is solid metal. How can there be water inside it?"

"It smells as septic as the sea." Zill shrugged. "Well, the seaweed won't mind, I'm sure. Come on, Fur-boy, let's tell Dolofin his high-rise larder is ready and get him looking for Danjo."

"Wait," Plog hissed. He'd just glimpsed movement somewhere above them in the dark and caught a strange, sweaty smell on the night air – quickly followed by a furtive, scuttling sound. "I think I heard something . . ."

"Something like this?" came a throaty snarl above him. The next moment, two white, pongy, maggoty creatures dropped down into sight. Their thick arms ended in even thicker fists, and their eyes burned angry red. Before Plog and Zill could even react, the maggot monsters jumped forward – and attacked!

"Whoa!" gasped Plog as his attacker grabbed him by the snout. "Where did you spring from?"

"You'll soon see," growled the other maggot-man. "We've been sent to take you there."

"Don't think so," Zill snarled, pushing back her attacker with a swipe of her tail. As he returned to the attack, she spat out a slime-line like a tripwire at ankle-height. The maggot-man fell over it, landing with a clang.

At the same time, Plog managed to shove away his own assailant, then he raised the giant slime-shooter to cover both maggot-men. "Thanks for the exercise," he growled. "Now, who are you?"

"I'm Marvin," said the biggest one.

"I'm Maynard," his friend added. "And there's a very unfriendly squid just behind you . . ."

"What?" Plog and Zill turned quickly – only to find there was nothing there. And while they were distracted, the maggot monsters pounced!

WHUMP! Plog was knocked to the floor by a sock to the jaw from Marvin. He banged his head on the metal and the world seemed to erupt in stars. Then he heard Zill struggling furiously in Maynard's clutches.

Must help her, Plog thought desperately, trying to reach for the fallen bazooka. But his body would not respond.

"Take them to the control centre,"

Marvin snarled. It was the last thing Plog heard before blackness closed over his throbbing head . . .

Meanwhile, in the lav-lab, Furp was running tests on the scrap of squid tentacle and the cloudy goo he'd found in the seawater. "How very curious," he murmured, comparing the two. "They are both made from the same stuff – only one is solid, and one is liquid. How can that be?" He scratched his head under his crash helmet, trying to puzzle things out. "Now, the goop appeared when the squid *dis*appeared, just as Plog turned on the Slime-mobile's headlights." He frowned. "Come to think of it, the squid disappeared before when I boosted the Slime Sub's headlights. I wonder . . ."

"Ahoy there, Furp!" Dolofin's voice floated in from outside. "Us heard some funny noises from up yonder in them cliffs. And us can't be seeing no sign of Zill or Clog."

"Plog," Furp corrected him, opening the door. "That's funny. They know we're in a hurry to find Danjo and the sub — and I've got a quite incredible theory about these squid I want to share with them. Why would they go wandering off?"

A little anxiously, Furp hopped over to the cliff face and used his slimy hands and feet to scale the smooth metal surface. Dolofin followed more slowly using the slime net.

In the soft glow from the junkjack's skin, Furp looked around the empty cave. "Plog! Zill!" he cried, but only a mournful, metallic echo carried back to him. The slime bazooka lay on the ground, together with a handful of Plog's fur and hairs from Zill's bushy tail. "Oh, dear. I fear something may have happened to them." Stepping forward, Furp saw that water had pooled in the bottom of the crater.

"Where did that come from?" Dolofin wondered.

"I don't know." Furp used his crash helmet as a bucket to bail out the water. "There's something at the bottom of this puddle, squashed into the ground." He went on ladling away.

"It's . . . it looks like a cork!" He pulled a magnifying glass from his pants and beckoned Dolofin to cast a little more light. "Very interesting. A cork sticking out of a solid metal cliff in a puddle of water."

"Zill and Bog must have plopped it in there," said Dolofin.

"No, no, no." Furp shook his head, peering through the magnifying glass. "There are tiny metal splinters on the top of this cork – and scratches on the side. Which suggests to me this cork was pushed up from *inside* the cliff face!"

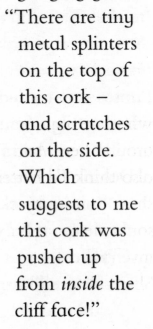

"What?" Dolofin's nose curled in confusion. "How could anyone push a cork up from inside the cliffs? They be solid metal."

"Remember those strange rumbles and vibrations you heard in these Cast-Iron Cliffs? I don't think we can put them down to cast-iron mice . . ." Furp nodded thoughtfully. "You know, I think I'm starting to understand what's really going on around here. And I also think I'd better show you junkjacks some clever stuff I've invented called Slime-Power Plus . . ."

★

73

Some time later, Plog woke with an aching head and opened his eyes. *Where am I?* He frowned – it was still dark. Had his eyes stopped working?

"Fur-boy?" whispered Zill, somewhere close by. "Are you OK?"

"I have the world's biggest headache," he muttered. "How about you?"

"Those maggot things hit me pretty hard," said Zill. "When I stopped seeing stars I found we were here, tied up in the dark."

Listening to Zill speak, Plog realized there was a strange, metallic echo to her words. He could hear water lapping close by, and a powerful electric hum. "Those maggots said they were taking us to a control centre. But where?"

"Inside the Cast-Iron Cliffs, as it happens!" came a shrill squawk from somewhere close by. A smellyvision set – like a kind of TV, only whiffier – flickered on nearby to present a sinister,

74

shadowy form. Part bird, part demon, part who-knew-what, the misshapen figure puffed itself up, its true features hidden from view. "Welcome," it rasped, "to my most secret and deadly lair of all . . ."

"I know that voice." Plog closed his eyes and groaned. "It's Lord Klukk!"

Chapter Seven
HIGH TIDE AND LOW-LIFES

"Greetings, *buk-buk*-bear-rat!" Lord Klukk hissed, peering out from the smellyvision set. "Good day, poodle-skunk!"

"It *was* a good day till I saw you, pants-head," Zill retorted.

"We guessed you'd be involved in this business somehow, Klukk," said Plog. "Why are you trying to scare away the junkjacks? And what do you mean, we're inside the Cast-Iron Cliffs?"

"Turn on the safety lights, my maggoty minions," rasped Klukk. "Let our prisoners see my power and tremble!"

Marvin hit a switch, and dim red lights flickered on in the solid metal ceiling not far above their heads. Plog saw that he and Zill were tied up on a kind of long platform made of wire mesh and crammed with strange machinery, sticking out from the wall.

He gasped as he realized just how vast this secret lair really was — bigger than fifty monster-football stadiums put together. And the entire place was filled with dark, evil-smelling water.

77

If the level rose much higher it would be lapping at the platform.

Plog looked at Klukk's image. "Aren't there easier ways to get your own indoor swimming pool than hollowing out the biggest range of cliffs in Trashland and pumping them full of water?"

Lord Klukk gave an unpleasant laugh. "This is no mere swimming pool. This water will *buk-buk*-bring me power over Trashland."

"You've tried to get power over Trashland before," Zill shot back. "We always stop you."

"But this time I shall *buk-buk*-be victorious," clucked Klukk. "While you shall perish at the many tentacles of a radio-actipus!"

78

Plog boggled. "A radio-*what*-i-pus?"

"I invented the name myself," said Klukk grandly. "It is short for 'radioactive octopus' – what you could call a supernatural squid." He laughed again. "These wonderfully revolting creatures will make me triumphant over all . . ."

"Creatures?" Zill gulped. "We thought there was only one that kept disappearing and reappearing, like a ghost."

Marvin smirked. "Them squid can't vanish and come back again, silly lady!"

"We've seen them disappear with our own eyes," Plog retorted.

"It is you two who will disappear," said Klukk, changing the subject. "I like to reward my squiddy servants with an extra tasty treat now and then." He leaned forward, sniggering. "I sent one to swallow up that silly sub with your friend on board . . . and soon I will let its friends feast on YOU!"

As Klukk laughed long and hard, Plog thought of Danjo being swallowed up and his heart sank deeper than the dark waters below the platform. By stretching out his fingers he could just reach one of Zill's paws and gave it a comforting squeeze. "I know things seem bad," he whispered. "But Danjo's tougher than any monster I've ever met."

Zill nodded. "And we're not finished yet."

"Marvin," Klukk commanded. "Summon the squid and activate the starv-o-matic aggravator."

"The what?" asked Zill as the maggot-man pressed a button.

Klukk sneered. "Why should I tell you?"

Plog glared at the screen. "Because you can't resist any opportunity to boast about how clever you are."

"Fair point," Klukk conceded. "Very well then – I'll tell you."

Plog leaned closer to Zill, his voice a low whisper. "And while he yabbers on, maybe we can untie these ropes and break free!"

Klukk cleared his throat. "While gathering toxic waste from the Radiation Reefs for my experiments, I discovered these remarkably unpleasant radio-actipuses. They not only live in water, they have the power to create it."

Zill was surprised. "They *make* water?"

"Tons of it," Klukk said happily. "It squirts out of their *buk-buk*-bottoms whenever they've eaten. Now, usually the *buk-buk*-beasts dwell down in the deepest depths and eat only a few scraps of seaweed – so they don't make much water."

"But the boss created a special transmitter," said Maynard. "The starv-o-matic aggravator. It sends a mind-controlling signal through the water that makes the squid extra-hungry and very aggravated."

"The signal forces them to go out hunting and come back here," added Marvin. "They just can't help themselves. Course, we have to keep it dark, 'cos the squid can't stand bright light, it makes them—"

"Silence!" roared Klukk, and the maggot-men cringed. "How dare you interrupt my evil explanation?"

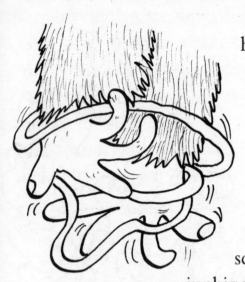

Plog, working his wrists free of his bonds, decided to interrupt too. "So that aggravator thing has made the squid go scoffing all the junkjacks' seaweed. And signalling through the water like that, I bet it's made the rest of the sea-life aggravated and hungry too."

Zill nodded. "So *that's* what turned the goopfish and jellyfish and the rest so cranky!"

"Yes, yes," said Klukk impatiently. "That is simply a side-effect of my squid-enslaving signal – the radio-actipuses are all that concern me. I can even direct them to follow simple instructions such as attack, destroy and gobble up . . . *Buk-buk*-but aren't you going to ask me why I want them to make so much water in the first place?"

Plog shrugged. "Because you get very thirsty?"

"No," said Klukk. "So I can flood half of Trashland with a deadly tidal wave whenever I choose!"

"Oh." Plog gulped. "That would've been my second guess."

"What do you mean, flood half of Trashland?" Zill demanded.

"My minions have built a tunnel stretching from the Septic Sea, underneath Pongo *Buk-buk*-Beach, and into these hollowed-out cliffs," Klukk hissed gloatingly. "The squid swim inside after feeding, squirt out their *buk-buk-*bottom-water and my demonic dams carefully contain it here. When the cliffs are full to *buk-buk-*bursting, I will announce my demands to the monsters of Trashland: they must worship me as their most wonderful ruler, or else I will detonate the many *buk-buk-*bombs I have stuck to the cliff walls to unleash a tidal wave and wreak widespread destruction . . ." He threw back his head and laughed uproariously.

Zill shuddered. She remembered the view from the cliffs – all the way from the Poo-nited States to the skyscrapers of Goo York. This mountain of water would flatten everything, monsters and buildings alike, whenever Klukk chose . . .

Then, suddenly, the dark waters below began to bubble.

For a brief moment, Plog and Zill dared to imagine it was Danjo coming to their rescue. But the next moment, a familiar, bloated form began to rise up, its murderous tentacles twitching with terrible intent. In the dim, blood-red light, the radio-actipus looked more terrifying than ever.

"Aha," said Klukk, "the squid I summoned has arrived! And he appears to *buk-buk*-be in a state of *dreadful* aggravation . . ."

He raised a shadowy wing and clicked his claws. "Marvin, Maynard – feed these slime-loving fools to our angry friend!"

"No!" shouted Zill, struggling furiously as Marvin picked her up.

Plog said nothing. He was close to freeing himself. All he needed was a few more seconds . . . But Maynard wasn't about to let him have them. With a gap-toothed grin he hauled Plog to his feet and shoved him over the platform's edge . . .

Chapter Eight

SHOWDOWN WITH THE SQUID

SPLA-SPLOOSH! Plog hit the freezing, smelly water a moment before Zill did. At once, thrashing tentacles rose up from the black water and stretched out towards them.

Plog finally tore his hands free. "Swim for it, Zill!"

"Only got two paws untied, Furboy," Zill panted.

"Save yourself. I'll try and distract it."

"No way," Plog shot back. "Hang onto me and we'll use your tail as an oar. Move!"

Zill scrambled onto Plog's back and they powered away through the water.

But the squid was seething with rage and horribly close behind them. Zill splashed with her tail, and Plog swam with all his might, but his iron boots were weighing him down. In desperation, Zill spat out a slime-line and tried to tie the squid's tentacles together — but the beast was too strong, and snapped the sticky rope apart.

"Swim all you like," yelled Marvin. "There's no way out."

"The radio-actipus will get you in the end," Maynard shouted.

The rubbery body of the deep-sea demon burst from the water, as big as the Slime-mobile, its beak snapping, its single eye narrowed with hatred.

"Turn your tail faster," Plog panted to Zill; his legs ached so much. It was all he could do to stay afloat. "We've got . . . to get . . . away . . ."

"Too late!" cried Zill. With Klukk and his maggot-men's laughter ringing in her ears, she closed her eyes as the supernatural squid towered over them and opened its jaws.

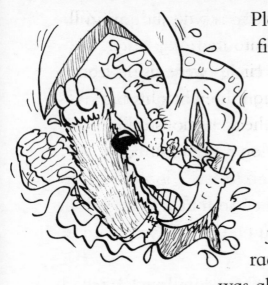

Plog raised his fists to the ravenous squid, determined to go down its throat fighting. But just as the radio-actipus was about to swallow the Squaddies – PLOOP! It disappeared, leaving nothing but cloudy gloop.

Zill gasped. "Why did it vanish just as it was about to eat us?"

"I don't know." Plog realized that Klukk's laughter had turned to babbling rage, aimed at his two hench-monsters.

"Fools!" spat the mastermind. "Nincompoops! What did you do?"

"*We* didn't make the squid explode, master," Maynard protested.

"Then maybe that thing did . . ." Zill pointed grimly into the inky water. Two glowing yellow circles were rising from the deeps, getting larger, brighter . . ."It's the eyes of another sea monster!"

"No, wait!" Plog pointed in amazement as a familiar gleaming craft rose into sight, its headlights beaming about the gloomy cavern. "It's the Slime Sub!"

A moment later, the roof hatch opened up – and Danjo emerged, grinning all over his face. "Plog and Zill – am I ever glad to see you!"

"Good to
see you too,
big guy!"
said Plog as
he and Zill
splashed over
to join the
crab-monster in
a soggy group hug.
"How did you get away from that squid
back at the beach? Klukk said it
swallowed you."

"It did," Danjo agreed, "just as I made
it inside the sub. Luckily, the sub's new
super-shielding kept me safe inside the
squid's belly – until it suddenly went
pop."

"But why did it go pop?" Plog
wondered.

"Arrrrgh!" screeched Lord Klukk.
"Those squalid Squaddies have more
lives than a nuclear-powered cat. Destroy
them, my maggot minions! And there are

more radio-actipuses on the way, so shoot out those headlights *buk-buk*-before they arrive or I will shoot YOU!"

"Orders received and understood, your Lordliness," said Marvin. He and Maynard pulled out big white guns and started blasting.

"Quick!" Danjo hauled Plog and Zill inside the sub.

At once, Zill jumped into the pilot's seat and pulled on a lever. "Taking us down!" she cried as the small craft dipped and descended.

But the next moment – BWAMM! A huge explosion went off in the water close by, rocking the sub.

"Marvin and Maynard have got bombs!" Plog groaned. "Probably the same explosives they've stuck to the sides of the cliffs, ready to flood Trashland."

"We must get out of here and warn Furp and PIE about Klukk's plans, pronto," said Zill.

"Especially with more squid on the way," Danjo agreed.

Plog held on tight as the sub accelerated. "Let's just hope Klukk doesn't open the floodgates in the meantime."

But suddenly he saw a bomb float down in front of the windscreen. "Reverse, Zill!" he yelled.

But it was too late. A colossal muffled crash tore through the water! For a moment, the black depths shone red-orange and the sub was smashed backwards, spinning wildly. Plog, Zill and Danjo were hurled around like marbles in a tin. The controls blew out completely – and as the shockwaves stopped, so too did the whine of the little craft's engines.

"No power," groaned Zill. "Now we're a sitting target for any passing radio-actipus!"

97

"And I don't want to worry you," said Danjo. "But here come three of them right now!"

Plog swallowed hard as he saw the massive, billowing shapes come streaking out of the darkness towards them, a mass of flailing tentacles. "Even Furp's new defences won't keep this lot out! They're going to . . ."

PLOOP! PLAP! PLURP!

In an explosion of goo, the savage squid suddenly exploded.

The Squaddies stared in baffled amazement as twenty points of bright green light came sparkling into view through the thick, goopy water.

"More bright lights," Plog breathed.

"Must belong to more sea monsters." Danjo gulped. "They might be even nastier than the squid."

"We'll soon find out," said Zill as the dazzling lights grew larger and brighter still. "They're heading straight for us!"

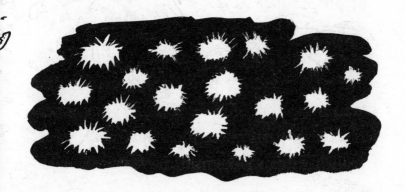

Chapter Nine

THE ALLIES ATTACK!

Suddenly, a neon-green shape slithered across the Slime-sub's windscreen. "Look out!" yelled Plog. The shape shone so brightly, he had to shield his eyes. Only once it had moved further away could the Squaddies make it out properly . . .

Zill laughed in amazement. "It's Dolofin!" The junkjack was glowing more intensely than an atomic lightbulb, and carrying something on his mega-bright back – a froggy monster in diving gear . . .

"FURP!" cheered Plog, Zill and Danjo.

Zill pointed to the other luminous figures. "They must be the other junkjacks." Plog scratched his head. "But what's happened to make them shine like that?"

Dolofin and three other junkjacks swam underneath the stranded Slime Sub and heaved it up towards the surface. As it broke through the black waters, Plog saw they had emerged just out of sight of Klukk's control platform.

Furp quickly climbed onto the roof, raised the hatch and slipped inside with Dolofin. Plog, Zill and Danjo hugged and high-fived them, although they could hardly see for the old junkjack's shining skin.

"You're so bright, you should come with a health warning," Zill declared. "Furp, what did you do to him?"

"Simple!" Furp grinned and pulled out a bottle of Slime-Power Plus. "My super goo boosted the junkjacks' natural glow-energy!"

"Just as it boosted the sub's headlights and engines before," Danjo realized. "But why did you give it to them?"

"To deal with the menace of the squid!" Furp beamed. "I worked things out, you see. Remember the cloudy stuff in the water that our tentacled terror left behind when it disappeared? It wasn't ghostly goo, eerie ectoplasm or supernatural slime. It was all that was

left of a squid that had just
EXPLODED!"

Plog, Zill and Danjo were so amazed,
their jaws
almost
bounced off
their feet.

"Those
creatures
live in the
darkest,
blackest
deeps of the
Septic Sea,
right?" Furp
went on.
"They must

be super-sensitive to light – *allergic* to it,
in fact. So allergic, that bright light
makes them explode!"

"Of course," said Plog with growing
excitement. "That's why it's so dark out
there – and why Klukk wanted his

maggot-men to shoot out our headlights." He turned to Zill and Danjo. "The first time we saw a squid disappear was when Furp boosted the sub's headlights with Slime-Power Plus, right? A different one grabbed us from behind, but it popped when we dragged it to the surface in bright sunshine."

"Right," Zill agreed. "And the Slime-mobile's headlights made that one by the shore go 'ploop'. But why did the

one that ate Danjo explode?"

"I couldn't figure out how to switch on the Slime Sub's headlights for ages," said Danjo sheepishly.

"I guess the brightness burned up its belly in the end . . ."

Furp nodded. "And once I'd realized that bright light was lethal to these squid I went to tell Plog and Zill – only to find that they'd disappeared and that the Cast-Iron Cliffs were leaking water! Of course, I had to find you . . ."

"So he brightened up us junkjacks with Slime-Power Plus and got us to hunt about for a secret way into the cliffs," Dolofin explained. "We saw a whole load of squid go through a hole in the seabed—"

"And it led us here," Furp concluded. "Judging by the clever devices that hold in all the water while the squid come and go, I'm guessing Lord Klukk is involved."

"Right up to his shadowy beak," Plog agreed. "We've got to smash his control centre."

Danjo smiled. "With ultra-luminous junkjacks to protect us from the squid, that leaves just two maggot-men out there to deal with."

"Armed with bombs, guns and the power to blow these cliffs apart and drown half of Trashland," said Zill.

"What?" Furp's eyes went extra boggly. "Then we must attack at once."

"I've got a plan," said Plog. "But it's not a very safe one."

"Is it ever?" Zill grinned. "Tell us more . . ."

One minute later, guarded by glowing junkjacks, Plog and Danjo were swimming underwater towards the control centre on the platform. Marvin and Maynard were staring into the water, guns raised, apparently confused.

"Well?" Lord Klukk squawked from his two-way smellyvision set. "Have you learned what caused the radio-actipuses to *buk-buk*-blow up?"

"They probably just ate too much," Maynard decided.

"Yeah," said Marvin. "That furry orange bear thing would give anyone indigestion . . ."

I'll give you a lot more than that, Plog thought darkly as he and Danjo quietly emerged below the platform, right under the maggot-men's feet. "Get ready, Danjo. Zill and Furp should begin their distraction any time . . . now."

Suddenly, across the cavern, the Slime Sub popped up into sight – with Zill and Furp hiding behind it.

"It's the Squad!" spluttered Klukk. "OPEN FIRE!"

At once, the two maggot-men sprayed the sub and the water around it with a hail of muck bullets.

"Now, Danjo," hissed Plog. "While they're making a racket . . ."

Danjo reached up with his hot pincer and used it like a tin opener to cut into the base of the platform, the sizzling slime within scorching through the thick wire mesh.

"Our bullets are bouncing off that sub thing," Marvin complained.

"Then use a *buk-buk*-bomb," raged Klukk. "Destroy that sub!"

"Quickly, Danjo," urged Plog.

"I'm going as fast as I can," grunted the crimson crab-monster, still hacking away.

Maynard hurled a bomb at the Slime Sub – and Zill's head popped up from the water. She spat out a slime-line and snagged the bomb in mid-flight – and with a jerk of her head she changed its course. BLAMMM! It exploded harmlessly in mid air. He threw another, and Zill dealt with it in the same way.

"She has blown up our last bomb," Marvin complained.

"That wretched poodle-skunk!" Klukk
clucked furiously. "Why have my squid
not squished her?"

"We'll take care of her now,"
Maynard growled, and raised his gun.
But suddenly,
Dolofin and his
twenty blinding
bright
junkjacks
jumped out of
the water,
splashing and
shouting in a
wide, protective
semicircle.

"Curse them all," Klukk roared as
Marvin and Maynard shielded their
eyes. "Faced with such *buk-buk-*
brightness, the squid won't be able to get
them. You must destroy those over-
luminous lump-heads, you miserable
maggots! Now. NOW!"

110

Like Maynard, Marvin hefted his white rifle – but then Furp came leaping out of the water, bouncing about from junkjack to junkjack, wiggling his butt and blowing raspberries. As he did so, the junkjacks ducked in and out of the water like performing seals.

Marvin waved his gun about helplessly. "Who do we aim at first?"

"I dunno," moaned Maynard.

"Get a grip, boys!" Zill spat another slime-line and used it as a whip, cracking at the maggot-men's fingers, trying to knock the guns away.

And while the noisy chaos raged on

all around, Danjo finally finished
cutting his hole in the base of the
platform. Taking a deep breath, Plog
pulled himself up through the jagged
gap. Marvin and Maynard didn't hear
him creeping up behind them . . .

"Let maggots disappear," Plog
boomed, "the Slime Squad is here!"

Marvin and Maynard turned round
in surprise − straight into a flying furry
fist. WHUMP! THUMP! The maggot
men went reeling over the control
centre's safety rail and fell with a
SPLASH into the water.

"Nooooo!" squawked Klukk,

quivering with rage
on the screen.

"'Fraid so,"
Plog told him
with a wink.
"And that's your
last line of
defence gone."

Danjo climbed
up to join him. "You
should know by now,
stinky beak – the power of slime will
win every time!"

"Nicely punched, Fur-boy!" Zill
called, swimming over as Dolofin and
the junkjacks grabbed Marvin and
Maynard in the water.

"Yes, indeed, Plog." Furp hopped out
of the water, his metal pants rattling.
"Now, let's deactivate all this terrible
equipment."

"Go ahead and try," sneered Klukk.

"I will, thank you." Furp pressed a

button on the main panel – but then a loud raspberry burst from the controls. They flashed on and off, and turned an angry red.

"Ha!" Klukk chortled. "I rigged the controls to self-destruct if anyone tried to work them without entering the proper code. And when they explode, the cliff walls will go with them. All this lovely water will devastate Trashland – and you silly slimy Squaddies will *buk-buk*-be to *buk-buk*-blame!"

Chapter Ten

CAST-IRON CATACLYSM

Klukk burst into noisy
laughter, and Danjo
crossly squirted
red-hot slime at
the screen. The
smellyvision set
blew up in a
cloud of smoke,
and an eerie silence
settled.

Plog turned to the maggot-men in
the water. "What *is* the proper code?"

"It's too late now," moaned Maynard.

"Once the self-destruct is set, there's
no way to stop it," Marvin agreed.

"I be thinking us had better push off sharpish!" Dolofin called – as the fierce glow about him faded. Soon he was back to his normal, softly glowing self.

"Uh-oh," said Furp as the other junkjacks started fading too. "The effect of the Slime-Power Plus is wearing off – and I haven't got any more."

"No lights means no way to keep back the squid," Zill murmured. "And that aggravator thing is still jammed on, driving them mad . . ."

"Terrific," Plog groaned. "As if things weren't bad enough already, the squid could attack at any moment – and we're completely defenceless!"

"We've got to destroy these controls," said Furp.

116

"The explosion that tears open these cliffs will destroy them all right," Danjo muttered.

"That's it!" boomed Plog. "At the end of the countdown, the bombs stuck to the cliff walls will explode. But if we can get one of those explosives now and use it to blow up the controls . . ."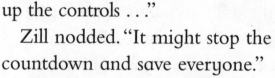

Zill nodded. "It might stop the countdown and save everyone."

"It's worth a try," said Furp.

Plog looked down at the maggot-men. "Where's the nearest bomb?"

"We'll never tell you," vowed Marvin.

Danjo pointed behind them, where the water was churning. "Look – the squid are coming!"

"In that case we *will* tell you." Maynard pointed to the far wall. 'They're over there, just below water level."

"And with aggravated squid coming, just below water level is not a good place to be," said Dolofin. As huge probing tentacles splashed through the water towards them, he and his crew splashed up onto the now-crowded platform. Marvin and Maynard clambered after them. The controls started flashing faster.

"How can we get the bomb now?" Danjo cried. "If we swim for it, the squid will get us."

Suddenly, a massive tentacle smashed into the side of the platform and several junkjacks almost fell into the water. "They'll get us if we stay here too," said Zill shakily.

Plog rounded on Marvin and Maynard. "How did you get me and Zill into this place?"

"We pulled you up to the top of the cliffs on ropes," said Maynard, "then brought you down here through a secret tunnel."

"It's here." Marvin banged on the wall and a jagged door slid open. "See ya!" Before anyone could stop them, he and Maynard sprinted through the doorway and were lost from sight.

Danjo was about to chase after the maggot-men when another super-tough tentacle thumped against the platform, knocking him down.

Everyone yelled in alarm as a giant squid snapped savagely at the safety rail.

Plog turned to Dolofin. "Lead your crew outside too," he said. "At least they'll be safe from the squid."

"Thanks, Nog." Dolofin herded the junkjacks into the tunnel. "And if you can stop us all from being blown sky-high, that would be nice!"

"Wouldn't it just," Plog muttered as the control panel started flashing even faster. Another tentacle smashed against the platform.

"This place can't last much longer," said Danjo.

"Zill." Plog looked at her. "It's dangerous, I know – but do you think you can swing across the cavern with Furp and reach that bomb?"

"It's no more dangerous than staying here," said Zill bravely. She climbed onto the safety rail at the platform's edge, took a deep breath, then spat a slime-line up at the high metal ceiling. It stuck! Furp hopped onto her back and grabbed hold of her tail. "Here goes nothing," she said – and launched herself across the cavern!

Plog watched anxiously as she and Furp hurtled through the air.

When Zill reached the end of her swing, Furp jumped off, his momentum carrying him all the way to the far wall in a matter of seconds.

"Made it!" he cried, and started scuttling down towards the bomb below the water.

Zill, meanwhile, swung back towards the balcony – but before she could reach safety, a tentacle burst from the water and plucked her out of the air! The vile, baggy body of a gigantic squid rose up out of the water, its single bloodshot eye narrowed . . .

"Zill!" Plog dived off the balcony, landing right on the squid's squelchy eyeball with his iron boots!

With a shriek, the
squid convulsed
and hurled Zill
away – straight
into Danjo's
arms. But Plog
was left
clinging onto
the squid's
horrible head – and
more of the monsters were
coming towards him . . .

"I've got the bomb!" Furp cried,
clinging to the wall above the water,
waving a round, black device.

"And I've got trouble," Plog realized,
perched precariously on the furious
squid.

Zill frantically coughed up a slime-
strand. "Catch hold, Fur-boy!"

Plog grabbed hold of Zill's sticky rope
and swung back to the platform just as
several squid tried to chomp him in two.

At the same time, Danjo shot a freezing jet of slime across the cavern that hardened to form an icy bridge. "Furp, get your skates on – slide, boy, slide!"

Furp jumped onto Danjo's slimy ice-slide and skidded clear across the divide, dodging flailing tentacles, clutching the bomb in both hands.

No sooner had he collapsed onto the platform than the slide was smashed to bits by another seething squid.

"Nothing like cutting it fine," joked Furp feebly, getting to his feet.

"Here!" Plog took the bomb in trembling hands and placed it on the

control panel, now flashing about a
million times a second. Zill stuck the
explosive in place with a swiftly spun
slime-net.

"Danjo," Plog panted. "Squirt that
explosive with enough hot slime to set it
off – and then everybody run."

"Understood," said
Danjo. Taking careful
aim, his three legs
holding him steady
even as the squid
pounded at the
platform again,
Danjo squirted a jet
of boiling slime at the
bomb's black casing. It
began to steam . . .

"RUN!" Plog bellowed, shooing his
friends away. The four of them ran
along a steep cast-iron tunnel, black
as pitch and winding steeply upwards.
The ground trembled beneath them.

Iron filings dropped from the roof.
Finally, the four Squaddies burst out
into bright morning sunlight and—
FA-BOOOOOM!
The bomb went off right on top of
the control panel. The shockwaves shook
the clifftops! Dolofin and his junkjacks
were thrown to the ground. Plog, Zill,
Furp and Danjo all clung to each other,
hoping against hope that they had
stopped the deadly countdown and not
simply kick-started the destruction of
the cliffs and the ultimate trashing of
Trashland . . .

But finally, the shockwaves subsided. As the last tremors faded, the Cast-Iron Clifftops held steady and still.

Plog raised his head and peered all about. "We're still here!"

"It worked." Zill grinned. "The water's still inside the cliffs. Your nutty plan worked, Fur-boy!"

The junkjacks cheered, and the Squaddies breathed an enormous sigh of relief.

Furp hopped over to the cliff edge. "Look!" he said, pointing down way below to the Septic Sea.

Joining him, Plog saw a horde of shadows beneath the water, fading from sight.

"The so-called supernatural squid," he murmured. "Finding their way back home."

Zill nodded. "Now the aggravator's gone up in smoke, they'll be back to normal – eating just a little and staying out of sight."

Danjo looked round at the junkjacks, whose cheeks were oddly full. "Hey, what are *you* eating?"

"Just a bit of seaweed," said Dolofin. "Us found quite a lot of it growing in the water in them cliffs," said another junkjack, also munching.

"Enough to feed all us junkjacks till they grow back in the Septic Sea," said Dolofin happily. "I'll be able to send for our families from abroad. Pongo Beach

128

and
the Septic
Sea will be our
true and proper home
once more."

A ragged cheer went up from
the munching junkjacks, and the
Slime Squad joined in with the happy
cries.

"It's a shame Marvin and Maynard
got away," Plog said sadly. "They might
have been able to tell us where to find
Lord Klukk."

Zill shuddered. "I have a feeling we'll
be seeing him again soon – *and* whoever
he's hired as his horrible helpmates."

"But until then . . ." Danjo pulled a pair of shades from his shorts. "How about a quick sunbathe?"

"Yes!" Zill stretched out on the warm iron and beamed. "This is the perfect place to top up my tan."

"The view's good too," said Furp happily, staring out over the world they'd saved.

"It certainly is," Plog agreed. "And the Slime Squad will go on fighting to keep Trashland just the way it is – wild, whiffy, and all-round wonderful!"

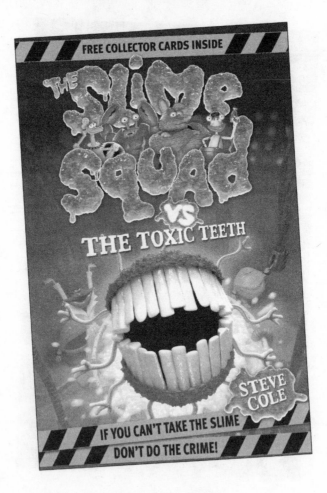